SHIVERWOOD ACADEMY
FRANKENSTEVE

Spellbound

An Imprint of Magic Wagon
abdobooks.com

by Lea Taddonio

To Jarah, Bronte and Poppy-I love you all best - LT

abdobooks.com

Published by Magic Wagon, a division of ABDO, PO Box 398166,
Minneapolis, Minnesota 55439. Copyright © 2020 by Abdo
Consulting Group, Inc. International copyrights reserved in all
countries. No part of this book may be reproduced in any form
without written permission from the publisher. Spellbound™ is
a trademark and logo of Magic Wagon.

Printed in the United States of America, North Mankato,
Minnesota.
052019
092019

 THIS BOOK CONTAINS
RECYCLED MATERIALS

Written by Lea Taddonio
Edited by Bridget O'Brien
Art Directed by Candice Keimig

Library of Congress Control Number: 2018964643

Publisher's Cataloging-in-Publication Data

Names: Taddonio, Lea, author.
Title: Frankensteve / by Lea Taddonio.
Description: Minneapolis, Minnesota : Magic Wagon, 2020. | Series: Shiverwood academy
Summary: Steve worries he won't be able to perform his hip-hop routine in his school
    talent show because he's an undead boy made of sewn together body parts, but his
    stage fright might be holding him back instead.
Identifiers: ISBN 9781532135019 (lib. bdg.) | ISBN 9781532135613 (ebook) | ISBN
    9781532135910 (Read-to-Me ebook)
Subjects: LCSH: Zombies--Juvenile fiction. | Hip-hop dance--Juvenile fiction. |
    Talent shows--Juvenile fiction. | Stage fright--Juvenile fiction. | Fear in
    children--Juvenile fiction.
Classification: DDC [Fic]--dc23

TABLE OF CONTENTS

Chapter One
THE TALENT
SHOW

Shiverwood students CROWD around the main door. I turn down the volume on my phone's music app and *tug* off my headphones.

"What's going on?" I ask

Azriel, a cute girl from my

History of SPOOKS class.

She's jumping up and down so

hard that her pointy witch hat

slides sideways.

"It's posted!" She **shrieks** before grabbing her broom and **ZOOMING** into the air. "Weeeeeee! I can't wait!"

"Madam Asp hung the sign-up sheet for the school **TALENT** show!" My friend Zeb **RUNS** up. "What're you going to do?"

I SHRUG. "That doesn't sound
like my thing."
Zeb SLUGS my arm.
"But everyone has a TALENT!
Even you."

"Watch out!" My arm TUMBLES
to the sidewalk. "Look what
you did."

"Sorry buddy," he says. "It's all
my super ZOMBIE strength!"

"It's fine," I mutter, scooping it
up. "I keep a needle and thread in
my locker for EMERGENCIES."

As I walk away, I hear people _giggling_ behind my back. I force my lips into a **FAKE** smile, but nothing about my life is funny.

Here at Shiverwood Academy

there are everything from

goblins to **VAMPIRES**.

But I'm the only kid that's an **experiment**. My parents are mad scientists who *SEWED* me together from body parts they dug out of cemeteries.

If I'm not *careful*, I can lose a hand or a leg. Once during a dodgeball game, my head got **KNOCKED** off!

But as I SEW my arm back on, I get a little idea. And all day long that little idea GROWS bigger and bigger.

What if I did sign up for the TALENT show? I love hip-hop. I could choreograph a dance routine.

This might be my chance to go from "Frankensteve the FREAK" to "Frankensteve the Fly."

Chapter Two
PRACTICE MAKES PERFECT

That night I **SHOVEL** pizza into my mouth as fast as I can. I can't wait to work on my hip-hop routine.

"*Slow* down, pal." Dad wipes his mouth with a napkin. "You don't want your tongue coming **loose** again."

A loud crash shakes the ceiling.

"Oh no!" Mom jumps up.

Her lab is in the attic. "The slime

must have EXPLODED.

I'll be right back." She's always

working on a crazy experiment.

"May I be excused?" I say,

PUSHING back my seat. "I'll

be in the garage doing some . . .

um . . . homework."

"*Mmmm-kay*." Dad doesn't look up from his newspaper.

Out in the garage, I crank up my favorite song and in no time at all I'm popping and locking. Out here I can forget everything that's wrong with my life. I feel good in my skin, not like a mixed-up collection of body parts.

After an hour I'm **sweaty** and breathing hard. But I also have choreographed a *KILLER* dance routine. I close my eyes and imagine my classmates giving me a standing **ovation**.

This is going to be **great**!

Chapter Three

STAGE FRIGHT

"This is going to be *terrible*," I whisper.

I'm backstage behind the theater curtains. Everyone trying out for the **TALENT** show is way better than me.

One kid played his violin. A girl JUGGLED eight shrunken heads. A ghost from my math class built a **HUGE** house of cards.

How can my dance COMPETE?

My legs feel like jelly. My heart races. My vision goes BLURRY. It's hard to swallow. If I step foot on that stage then I'll be laughed all the way to Transylvania.

"I gotta get out of here." I take a step backward and CRUNCH on something.

"*OUCH*! That's my foot!"

I spin in the direction of the girl's voice. Just my luck. I stomped on Azriel, the cute witch that I sort of have a crush on.

"**SORRY**, I was just leaving,"
I mumble.

"Hey, not so fast!" She **GRABS** my shoulder and holds me in place. "Where do you think you're going?"

"I . . . uh, **forgot** that I have to write a paper on the History of **SPOOKS**."

Azriel crosses her arms. "That paper was due last week. We're in the same class, remember?"

Then she *frowns*. "You look really sweaty. Are you sick or something?"

"No . . . I just . . . I just . . ." No believable lie pops into my brain. Time to go. "Excuse me."

I push past Azriel and RUN out of the school and into the graveyard. I SLUMP against a headstone. What a mess.

"Steve? Steve!" Azriel appears.

"Hey, can I talk to you for a second?"

 "Leave me alone." My voice

shakes like I'm about to

burst into tears any second. "You

don't understand."

She gives me a sad smile.

"Actually, I think I do."

Chapter Four
LIVING THE DREAM

I *roll* my eyes. "What do we have in common? You're **PERFECT**. I'm just pieces of a kid."

"For a smart guy, you're not acting very SMART. Do you remember that book report we had to give last month?"

I SHRUG. "Sure. Whatever."

"I was so *SCARED* to read mine that I almost threw up. My legs shook the whole time."

"Why? There's NOTHING wrong with you!"

"There's nothing wrong with you either. In fact . . ." She fidgets with her dress. "You're pretty cute. I was wondering if you'd be my date to the Monster Mash?"

"R-r-r-r-eally?" I can't believe my ears. Azriel wants me to be her date?

"Yep. On one condition. You go out on that stage and be your awesome self.

DEAL?" She holds out her hand.

I shake it. "**DEAL**."

"Now go NAIL that audition."

43

Finally, I **STEP** on
the stage. Azriel is in the
front row. She *winks*
right as the music starts.

I close my eyes and give myself over to the **BEAT**. I don't quit until the song finishes. For a moment there's *silence*. Then . . . the room fills with applause. I give a **BiG** bow.

I did it!

I don't want to live my

FEARS, not when I can live my

dreams. And that's just

what I'll do from now on.